Bat and Sloth
Solve a Mystery

To Wendy and Andrea: it's no mystery why
I'm so happy to have you as my editors!—LK

To Rose and Aliyah—SB

Library of Congress Cataloging-in-Publication data
is on file with the publisher.

Text copyright © 2021 by Leslie Kimmelman
Illustrations copyright © 2021 by Albert Whitman & Company
Illustrations by Seb Braun
First published in the United States of America in 2021
by Albert Whitman & Company
ISBN 978-0-8075-0582-3 (hardcover)
ISBN 978-0-8075-0574-8 (ebook)
TIME TO READ® is a registered trademark
of Albert Whitman & Company.

Printed in China
10 9 8 7 6 5 4 3 2 1 RRD 24 23 22 21 20

Design by Valerie Hernández

For more information about Albert Whitman & Company,
visit our website at www.albertwhitman.com.

Bat and Sloth
Solve a Mystery

illustrated by
Seb Braun

Leslie Kimmelman

Albert Whitman & Company
Chicago, Illinois

A Loud Noise

It was early morning in the rain forest.
The sky was cloudy.
The day was warm and misty.
On a branch of a tall tree,
two best friends had just gone to sleep.

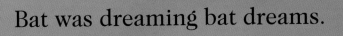
Bat was dreaming bat dreams.

Sloth was dreaming sloth dreams.

Suddenly there was a howl.
Bat almost fell off the branch.
"What was THAT?" he asked.
"Shh," murmured Sloth.
"I am trying to sleep over here."

Bat closed his eyes.

He tried to relax.

Another howl sounded:

WAAAAAHHH!

Sloth slowly opened one eye.

"What was THAT?" he asked.

Bat and Sloth looked all around the tree.

They looked left…and right.

They looked up…and down.

There! At the bottom of the tree!

"What is it?" Sloth asked his best friend.

"It's a…something," said Bat.

"Yes," agreed Sloth,
"but what kind of something?"
Bat looked. His eyes were not
very good.
He listened. His ears were *very* good.
"It's a *loud* something," he said.
"We need a closer look."

What Is It?

Bat flew down.
Ten minutes later,
Sloth arrived.
The loud something was crying.
But Sloth had a friendly smile.

Then the loud something saw Bat,
opened its eyes wide,
and got ready to scream.
Bat smiled.
He still looked scary.
But the loud something
seemed to know that Bat
was trying to help.

"We need to find out what it is," said Bat.
"And where it belongs.
It is all alone. Maybe it is lost."
"Yes," agreed Sloth. He yawned.
It was way past bedtime.
But the lost loud something needed them.
Someone somewhere was missing this
lost loud something. But who?
It was a mystery.

"It is certainly not a bat," observed Bat.
"No wings."
"It can't be a sloth either," said Sloth.
"It has hair, but just on top."

Sloth offered a banana.

The loud something gulped the fruit down.

It gulped down two more bananas.

"Maybe it is a monkey," said Sloth.
"Monkeys like bananas."
"Nope! No tail," said Bat.
"It cannot be a monkey."

An armadillo passed by.
"Armadillos have shells,"
Bat told Sloth.
"The loud something cannot be an
armadillo."
Sloth looked closely.

The loud something was very colorful.

"Maybe it is a toucan," he told Bat.

"No beak," replied Bat.

"So it is a toucan't."

Sloth smiled slowly.

His best friend was funny.

Good Cheer

The loud something looked sad.

"We need to cheer it up," decided Bat.

So Bat put on a show.

He did a loop-de-loop.

It was awesome.

The creature clapped and cheered.
Then *it* did a loop-de-loop!

Bat zipped and zapped.
The loud something clapped and
cheered again.
Then *it* zipped and zapped.

Bat and Sloth swung upside down
from the lowest branch of the tree.
So did the loud something.
"Whatever kind of animal you are,"
said Bat, "you are very talented."
The lost loud something made
some noise.
"I think that means it's feeling better,"
said Sloth. "I am not sure of every word."

"We still have to find out
where this loud something belongs,"
reminded Bat.
"I will fly up high
and see what I can see."

Bat flew up high.
Nothing he saw
looked like their new friend.
"Sorry," said Bat when he landed.
"We need a new plan."

The Found
Loud Something

The lost loud something said some words.

Bat and Sloth sort of, kind of understood.

But not completely.

Then they heard a loud noise.

"What was THAT?" asked Bat.

They heard the noise again.

This time Bat and Sloth listened carefully.

This is what Sloth heard: "CAAAAKE!"
He licked his lips.
This is what Bat heard: "SNAAAAKE!"
Oooh, Bat did not like that word.
Snakes were his least favorite animals.
This is what the loud something heard:
"JAAAAKE!"

The loud something jumped up
and began to run.
"IT'S ME! JAKE! I'M HERE!"
the creature shouted.
Zip! Zap! Zoom!

Jake ran into the arms of
two tall loud somethings.
"I'm glad it wasn't a snake," said Bat.
"You have snakes on the brain, Bat,"
said Sloth.
"Yes," agreed Bat.
"But I have Jake in my heart. Look!"

Sloth looked.
The three somethings
were hugging and kissing.

The found something turned back
to wave…
and wink.
Then it went on its way.

Bat and Sloth felt happy.
And Bat and Sloth felt sad.
Bat made up a song:
"His name was Jake.
He wasn't a snake.
To our tree he did roam.
Now he's on his way home."

"Nice," said Sloth.

Most of all, Bat and Sloth felt sleepy.

It was WAY past their bedtime.

The loud something had needed them,

and they had been there.

Now it was time to rest.

There were just a few hours to go

before the sun set,

before the moon rose,

before it was time to wake up

for a long, busy night.